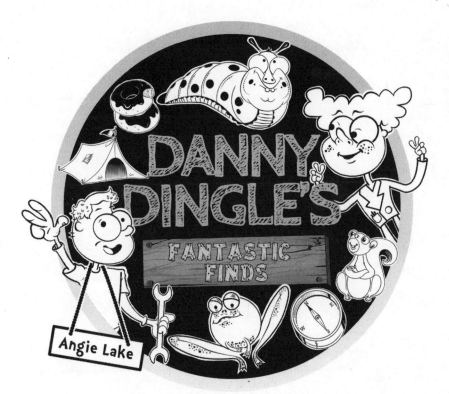

# The Super-Sonic
# Submarine

Published by Sweet Cherry Publishing Limited
Unit E, Vulcan Business Complex
Vulcan Road
Leicester, LE5 3EB
United Kingdom

www.sweetcherrypublishing.com

First published in the UK in 2016
ISBN: 978-1-78226-260-2

Illustrations © Creative Books
Illustrated by Shanith MM

Danny Dingle's Fantastic Finds: The Super-Sonic Submarine

Printed and bound by Thomson Press (India) Limited.

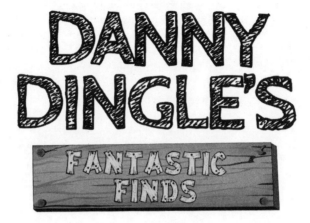

Book 2

# The Super-Sonic Submarine

Written by Angie Lake
Illustrated by Shanith MM

# DANNY DINGLE'S SUPER-SECRET SPY NOTEBOOK.

**DO NOT READ** (unless you are Danny, Percy or Superdog.)

It's for your own good.

**HONEST,** it is.

Why would I lie to you?

**BE WARNED:** If you turn the page, a giant caterpillar will crawl under your desk and be **SICK** on your toes!

TOLD YA !

Anyway,
This is me, **DANNY DINGLE.**

This is my best friend (and assistant),
# PERCY MCDUFF.

And this is my "pet", **SUPERDOG.**

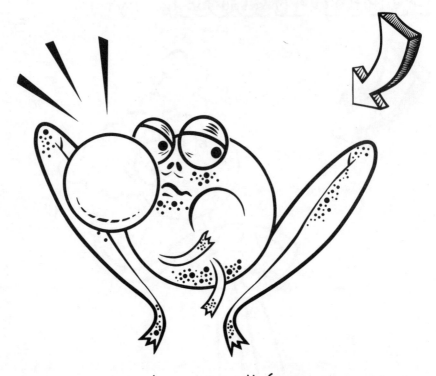

I tell people that he's my "pet" (Superdog, that is
– not Percy) but he's actually a (GENIUS) cleverly
disguised as a toad.

CLEVER, huh?

Percy, on the other hand, is just Percy.
He's not cleverly disguised as anything.

It's **REALLY** important that everyone goes on believing that Superdog is just a normal toad. If his cover is blown, he could be in

# LIFE-THREATENING DANGER!

Some people (Mum) are already TERRIFIED of his genius abilities and swat at him with a broom whenever he's around just in case he uses his *HYPNOTIC POWERS* on them.

So it seems only right that one  (me) should do what he can to try to protect the identity of another.

Percy, on the other hand, is just Percy.

Percy is **SICK**.
A lot.
And there's no escaping that.

This is a picture of Percy and I stood next to

# THE WORLD'S BEST SUPERHERO:

It was taken a few months ago at

Percy and I managed to get tickets to **METALWAY** by winning the Science Club Soap Box Derby last term in our fantastic **METAL-MOBILE!**

You see, Percy and I are **SUPER-INVENTORS** (at least, I am), and SMUG, FULL-OF-HIMSELF, TWIT-FACED Gareth Trumpshaw was no match for our (my) AWESOME - no, FARTSOME! - inventing powers!

(We **DEFINITELY DID NOT** just win because we were the only team left in the race . . .)

Winning those tickets was so important to Percy and me because we know that **METALWAY** is not only an AWESOME amusement park . . . it's also one of Metal Face's **SUPER-SECRET LAIRS!**

When we crossed that finish line and were handed our tickets, we knew that winning had been our FATE and that working for Metal Face was obviously our DESTINY

But when we got to Metalway, we spent so much time trying to find the secret entrance to the super-secret lair that we hardly had any time to go on any of the SUPER-COOL RIDES like:

# THE FARTINATOR!

# THE METAL-GO-ROUND!

# The PUDDING BREATH HOUSE OF HORRIBLE PUDDINGS!

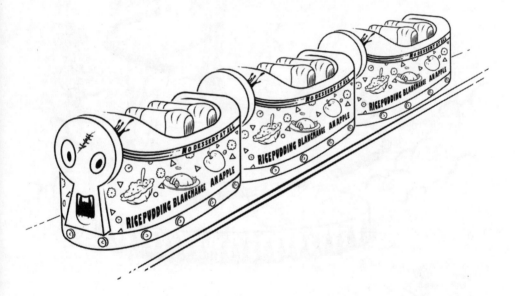

At least Superdog had a good time.

He was clever (as usual) and spent all day checking the **PUDDING BREATH** Vomit Flume for clues (flies).

We were getting pretty desperate (Percy was shouting secret passwords into a half-eaten ice cream cone) when I happened to glance up from a particularly **SUSPICIOUS-LOOKING** bin and saw . . .

# THE WORLD'S BEST SUPERHERO HIMSELF!

24

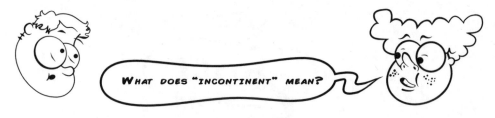

Going to **METALWAY** was a **LIFE-CHANGING EXPERIENCE** for us.

Percy and I have now decided that we will need to make **MUCH MORE** of an **EFFORT** on our inventing if we're going to go and work for Metal Face in his super-secret lair one day.

I mean, we ALL know that I am an **AMAZING SUPER-INVENTOR** already . . .

I'm **EXPERIMENTAL FACE**, remember?

(Don't pretend that you didn't already know!)

Hmm.

EITHER WAY, I know now that I'm going to have to step up my game if I want to become an IncontiNinja.

This can only mean one thing. . .—

# SPY TRAINING!

You see, Mr Hammond (teacher of Science/founder of Science Club/avoider of Ms Mills) let us in on a SUPER-SECRET during class the other day.

He said that there's a SUPER-SECRET SPY CLUB in Greenville that gets together EVERY WEEK to invent things, experiment and do "crafts"! (Percy says this means learning to be CRAFTY, not knitting and using glitter glue.)

According to Mr Hammond, they call themselves the **S.C.O.U.T.S.** (Spy Club Only for Ultra-Terrific Spies, or so I assume) so as not to draw attention to their **SUPER-SECRET SPY ACTIVITIES!**

Percy and I didn't know how Mr Hammond could have known this if this spy club was *SO* super-secret . . .

Percy and I didn't know whether this super-secret spy club knew that Mr Hammond was telling EVERYONE their super-secrets . . .

What Percy and I **DID** know was that **THIS WAS THE CLUB FOR US!**

This is **ULTRA-TERRIFIC SPY OVERLORD** (sorry – "Scout Master") Geoffrey.

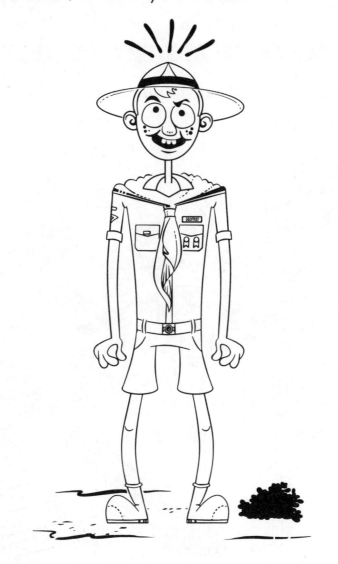

Admittedly, "Scout Master" Geoffrey doesn't look much like a spy trainer to the untrained eye . . .

In fact, I'd say that he looks more like a TRAIN SPYER, hahaha!

Y'know, those people who watch trains all day?

(Mum says that these people are actually known as TRAINSPOTTERS and that this EXCELLENT JOKE "doesn't really make any sense.")

(My parents ALWAYS ruin my excellent jokes.) Anyway, this is all just a SUPER-SECRET SPY TACTIC designed to confuse our parents into thinking that this is just some boring old kids club.

CRAFTY, huh?

But when Percy and I went to our S.C.O.U.T.S. induction meeting after school, "Scout Master" Geoffrey sat us down and told us that what was REALLY going on.

He showed us the S.C.O.U.T.S. secret handshake.

He even showed us the S.C.O.U.T.S. secret thumb trick!

(How did his thumb just come off like that?!)

Then he told us that as part of joining the S.C.O.U.T.S. we would get to work on lots of USEFUL and EXCITING things like:

## - PHYSICAL STUFF!

# EXPERIMENTAL STUFF!

# BUILDING STUFF!

He also said something about "*ethics*" and
"*commitment*" and "*initiative*" (huh?) but by
that point we were far too busy trying to work
out the secret thumb trick.

(I mean, HOW DID HIS THUMB JUST COME OFF
LIKE THAT?!)

Needless to say, Percy and I are now **SUPER-EXCITED**
for our **FIRST OFFICIAL** S.C.O.U.T.S. meeting
tomorrow!

We have since done ~~lots of~~, ~~some~~, almost **TWO WHOLE PRESS-UPS** in preparation!

. . . Maybe we will leave all of the physical stuff up to the other kids.

# WE HAVE BEEN LiED TO!

S.C.O.U.T.S. doesn't stand for "Spy Club Only for Ultra-Terrific Spies", and it isn't a super-secret spy club pretending to be "just some boring old kids club" . . .

This is all **DEFINITELY** Percy's fault.

A TRUE genius (like SUPERDOG) would've known about the old Scout neckerchief that Mr Hammond always wears under his shirt!

I can't BELIEVE that he was fooled by ONE stupid little thumb trick . . .

TYPICAL.

All we did all day at so-called "spy training" today was:

- Play rounders

- Get pushed down a hill on a desk chair by some of the older kids when Scout Master Geoffrey wasn't looking

# - Play rounders

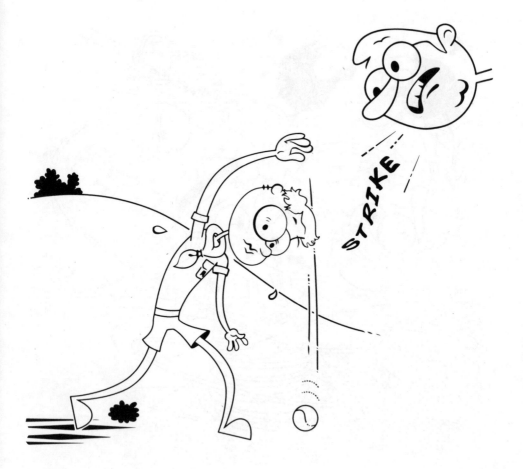

\- Boil spaghetti and tie knots in it (this made Percy sick, of course)

- Play rounders (again. . .)

I was feeling pretty tired and miserable after all of this horrible **EXERCISE** (BLEURGH!) on a Saturday morning (DOUBLE BLEURGH!) and was about to show Percy a secret thumb trick of my very own (I call it the "Licking My Thumb and Sticking it in Percy's Ear" trick) when Scout Master Geoffrey announced that the Greenville Association of Scouts was organising a **CAMPING TRIP!**

That meant:

-   No parents!

-   No school!

-   No SMUG, FULL-OF-HIMSELF, TWIT-FACED Gareth Trumpshaw!

HURRAY for Scouts! HURRAY! HURRAY!

Scout Master Geoffrey said that we'd get to practice everything that we'd learnt so far at Scouts . . . but in the **WILD!**

That means that we'll be able to do ALL SORTS of things, like . . .

Play rounders . . . in the **WILD!**

-   Get pushed down a hill on a desk chair by some of the older kids when Scout Master Geoffrey isn't looking . . . in the **WILD!**

- Play rounders . . . in the **WILD!** (again. . .)

- Boil up spaghetti and tie knots in it . . . in the **WILD!** (hopefully Percy can control himself)

- Play rounders . . . in the **WILD!**

I really hope that some of the other Scouts have had more than two and a half hours of spaghetti-knotting training, otherwise I'm pretty sure that WE'RE ALL (probably) *GOING TO DIE* . . . in the **WILD**!

Scout Master Geoffrey then handed us all a consent form and told us that we would need to get our parents to sign it before we would be allowed to go camping.
Wait, CONSENT FORM?

. . . Hang on.

"Greenville Association of Scouts"?

Hahaha, G.A.S. Camp!

Hmm . . . that gives me an idea . . .

It wasn't easy getting Mum to sign my consent form.

I think that she was still suffering from "**disappointment**" after my "**disappointing**" grades last year made her feel "**disappointed**".

REPORT CARD

ENGLISH **D⁻**

HISTORY **F⁻**

MATH **D⁻**

SCIENCE **A⁺**

I still think that this was a bit **UNFAIR** considering all of the effort that I put into keeping my egg from cracking in the Science Club challenge last term.

(I mean, come on – look how **BiG** that **A+** is!)

But, being the GENIUS that I am, I decided that the best course of action would be to bring the subject up over DINNER.

This is **ALWAYS** the best time to ask my mum for things because she's too busy chewing and feeding my baby sister, Mel. So she finds it harder to shout at me.

(This doesn't mean that she won't still try.)

# NOTE:

1. Tell Percy and Superdog this interesting idea.
2. Don't tell Mum I liked her idea.

Dad: Come on, Gwen – I was a Scout when I was a boy, and just look at how I've turned out!

Mum: Thank you, Steve – my point exactly.

(Great – thanks, Dad . . .)

Mum was distracted now anyway because Mel gurgled and did a little baby fart. She smiled and started cooing over her slobbery baby face.

I find this *particularly offensive*. Whenever I fart, Mum either rolls her eyes or makes me stand outside until I've "learnt to be civilised".

So, seeing as I was getting nowhere using my patented ASK MY MUM FOR THINGS OVER DINNER BECAUSE SHE'S TOO BUSY CHEWING AND FINDS IT HARDER TO SHOUT AT ME strategy, I decided to leave it until after tea when Mum was doing the WASHING UP.

Mum always **SAYS** that she hates washing up, but whenever Superdog and I try to help (Superdog likes to lick the plates clean) she **ALWAYS** snatches them back and cleans them again.

So I crept up on her like the **SUPER-SPY** that I am (no thanks to Scouts!) and tried a tactic that I have been working on for some time now.

One that requires *stamina, subtlety, intellect* . . .

Danny: Can I go to Scout Camp? Can I? Can I?
Can I? Can I? Can I? Can I? Can I? Can I?
Can I? Can I? Can I? Can I? Can I? Can I?
Can I? Can I? Can I? Can I? Can I? Can I?
Can I? Can I? Can I? Can I? Can I? Can I?
Can I? Can I? Can I? Can I? Can I? Can I?
Can I? Can I? Can I? Can I? Can I? Can I?
Can I? Can I? Can I? Can I? Can I? Can I?
Can I? Can I? Can I? Can I? Can I? Can I?
Can I? Can I? Can I? Can I? Can I? Can I?
Can I? Can I? Can I? Can I? Can I? Can I?
Can I? Can I? Can I? Can I? Can I? Can I?
Can I? Can I? Can I? Can I? Can I? Can I?
Can I? Can I? Can I? Can I? Can I? Can I?
Can I? Can I? Can I? Can I? Can I? Can I?
Can I? Can I? Can I? Can I? Can I? Can I?
Can I? Can I? Can I? Can I? Can I? Can I?
Can I? Can I? Can I? Can I? Can I? Can I?
Can I? Can I? Can I? Can I? Can I? Can I?

THAT IS **NOT** GOING
TO WORK WITH ME,
DANIEL GARFIELD DINGLE!

This was Mum's usual tactic.

## The DREADED MIDDLE NAME.

It takes me a few minutes to recover. But what kind of GENIUS would I be if I let something as stupid as GARFIELD (shudder) bother me. . .?

BUT JUST **THINK**, MUM
I'LL BE GONE FOR
A **WHOLE** WEEKEND . . .

I'VE ALREADY TOLD Y—WAIT. DID YOU SAY A WHOLE WEEKEND?

YEAH, BUT DON'T WORRY I THINK DAD SAID THAT HE HAD A NEW RECIPE FOR PICKLED EEL JELLY. I'M SURE THAT I COULD JUST SPEND THE WHOLE WEEKEND TESTING THAT WITH PERCY INSTEAD . . .

So I was feeling pretty pleased with myself when I met Percy to go to our Scout meeting, my signed consent form scrunched carefully in my back pocket.

I asked Percy how he'd got on asking his parents for permission.

He looked at me in the same way that I look at my maths homework (**BAFFLED**) and said that all he'd had to do was ask.

**WHAT?**

Percy's parents NEVER think that he's going to do anything STUPID or DANGEROUS.

Then again, I suppose HIS parents have never had to dig his head out of a rabbit hole like mine have . . .

(I was trying to prove to Superdog that underground lairs were great for keeping out intruders!)

Anyway, we kept an eye out for any COOL STUFF that we could use for inventing things on our way there.

This was because, as we all know . . .

Rule for **iNVENTORS** #1: You must **ALWAYS** be on the lookout for **COOL STUFF** !

That's why I carry my **SUPER-SECRET, SUPER-SPECIAL** inventor's kit around with me **AT ALL TiMES!**

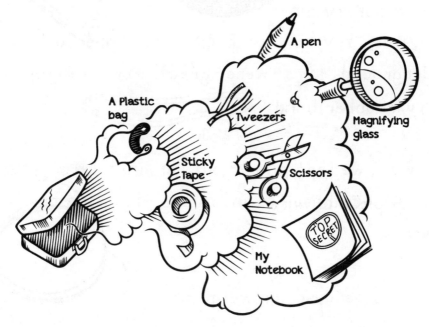

It contains:

A pen

A Plastic bag

Tweezers

Magnifying glass

Sticky Tape

Scissors

My Notebook

TOP SECRET

Inventor's Kit

Without my trusty inventor's kit, we might NEVER have managed to find:

- Half a pair of socks (one sock)

- A feather

- A safety pin

- A rubber band

- A piece of wire

This might not sound like much to those without my **iNVENTiVE GENiUS**, but I know that all of this **REALLY COOL STUFF** could come in handy for making . . .

Erm . . .

Oh, I know!

# A neck pouch for collecting EVEN MORE REALLY COOL STUFF!

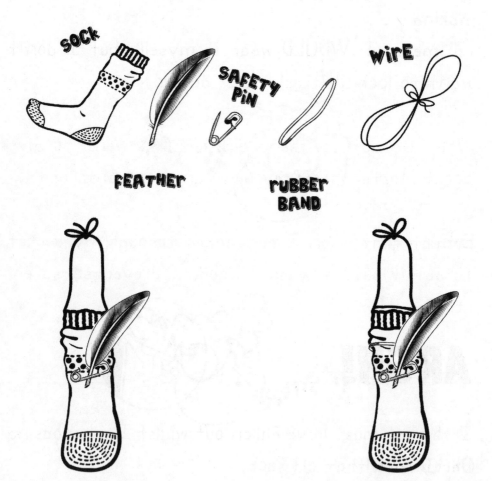

SOCK

FEATHER

SAFETY PIN

rubber BAND

wirE

Maybe I'll make one for Percy to wear later.

(I mean, I **WOULD** wear it myself, but I don't want to look RIDICULOUS, do I?)

When we got to the Scout hut, we went to give Scout Master Geoffrey our signed consent forms.

Except that when I rummaged through my pocket to get it out, it wasn't where I'd ever-so-safely stuffed it!

# ARGH!

I think it must have fallen out whilst I was chasing Percy with that old sock.

(You should've seen his face though – hahaha!)

So I quickly  scribbled my mum's name onto Percy's consent form and hoped that Scout Master Geoffrey would think that my mum had just signed his by accident.

He just took the form and stuffed it in his back pocket – he didn't even check them!

Typical.

Anyway, it turned out that there were only six of us going.

I assume that **PERSUASIVE SKILLS** are something that you must grow out of, because none of the older kids have even bothered trying to get their forms signed.

In fact, the ONLY ONES who'd brought back their consent form signed were the ones who'd joined at the same time as me and Percy because they had been too young to join before.

But even though the turnout was so low, Scout Master Geoffrey still seemed quite pleased.

I'm starting to suspect that Scout Master Geoffrey isn't actually very good at being a Scout Master . . .

How do I know this?

\-     He sometimes ties his neckerchief **SO TIGHT** that he can't breathe

\-     He sometimes **FORGETS** the words of the Scout Promise and just makes them up as he goes along

ON MY HONOUR,
I PROMISE THAT I WILL SHAVE MY CHEST.
TO DO MY DUTY TO DOGS AND THEIR FLEAS...

\-    He once set fire to a bucket . . . of sand

Mum thinks that he's "one sandwich short of a picnic", but then she also said that:

Mum: . . . you'd have to be to **VOLUNTEER** to put up with you lot every week!

I didn't hear this last bit at the time.

I was too busy thinking about picnics.

I like picnics.

Mmm, picnics . . .

Anyway,

At the end of the meeting, after doing lots of Scout
things (rounders, desk chairs, rounders, spaghetti
knotting, rounders), Scout Master Geoffrey gave
us a list of the things that we would need to take
with us:

# CLOTHING

- BANDANA OR HANDKERCHIEF
- SLIPPERS
- GLOVES (LINED)
- GLOVES/MITTENS (WARM)
- HAT (KNITTED)
- HIKING BOOTS (WATERPROOF)
- HIKING TROUSERS (LONG)
- JACKET
- LONG UNDERWEAR (MID WEIGHT)
- RAIN GEAR
- SHIRT (HEAVY)
- SHIRT (LONG SLEEVE), **2-3**
- SHIRT (SHORT SLEEVE) **2-3**
- SHOES (LIGHTWEIGHT)
- PYJAMAS
- SOCKS (HEAVY), **2-3** PAIRS (MORE IF WET OR SNOWY)
- UNDERWEAR
- JACKET/FLEECE

# GEAR

- BACKPACK
- COMPASS
- CUP
- EATING UTENSILS
- TORCH
- RUBBISH BAGS, **1-2**
- INSECT REPELLENT
- WHISTLE
- POCKET KNIFE (SMALL)
- WATERPROOF MATCHES
- PLASTIC PLATE AND BOWL
- NOTEBOOK AND PEN
- SCOUT BOOK
- SLEEPING BAG
- SLEEPING PAD
- SOAP
- SUN GLASSES
- WATER BOTTLE

## PERSONAL ITEMS

- FIRST AID KIT
- LIP BALM
- PRESCRIPTION MEDICATIONS
- SUNSCREEN
- WASH BAG
- TOWEL (SMALL)
- WATCH (WATERPROOF)

## DO NOT BRING:

- ELECTRONIC DEVICES
- BATTERY-OPERATED GAMES
- CD OR MP3 PLAYERS
- ETC.

## ABSOLUTELY NO PETS

I folded (crumpled into a ball) my packing list and safely put (stuffed) it away in my pocket (front pocket this time) before heading home with Percy.

Once we'd arrived back at my secret laboratory (I mean, **CLUBHOUSE!**) we'd managed to find EVEN MORE SUPER-COOL STUFF:

- A bent paperclip

- A broken belt

- A plunger

- Two nails

- Sticky tape

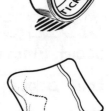

- A handkerchief

- A yoghurt pot

- String

As it had been such a **MASSIVELY** successful stuff-hunting day already, Percy and I decided to spend the rest of the afternoon working on a new invention based on a picture that we'd seen in our Scout handbook.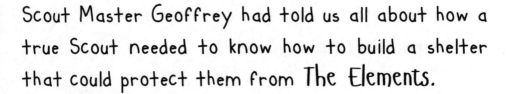

Scout Master Geoffrey had told us all about how a true Scout needed to know how to build a shelter that could protect them from The Elements.

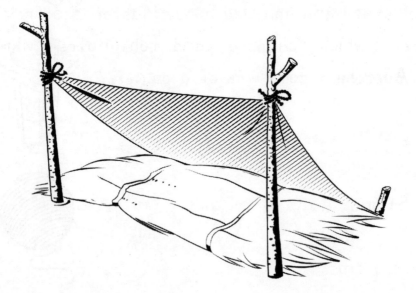

I don't think any of us knew why we would **EVER** need to build a shelter when we all have tents, or how exactly a sheet was supposed to be able to protect us from "The Elements" (or what exactly "The Elements" were supposed to be), but that didn't stop Scout Master Geoffrey jamming some sticks (which snapped) into the ground (which was hard) and tying a sheet (which tore) to them with rope (which came loose).

We all stood and admired Scout Master Geoffrey's shelter (which collapsed) and took notes (which were doodles – mine was of a picnic).

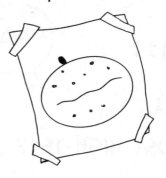

(Mmm, picnics . . .)

But, with all the LIFE-THREATENING DANGER that Superdog has to deal with on a day-to-day basis, I thought that it would be a good idea to use all of my newfound **KNOWLEDGE** to help protect him with a shelter of his very own.

GENIUS
AT
WORK
KEEP OUT

And now, with all these **COOL** new finds, I knew that Percy and I could build Superdog . . .

The **BIGGEST** . . .

OOOH!

The **BEST** . . .

AAAH!

*GASP*

The **MOST HIGH-TECH** . . .

# SPY SHELTER iN HiSTORY!

I set to work on an original (and very cool) design:

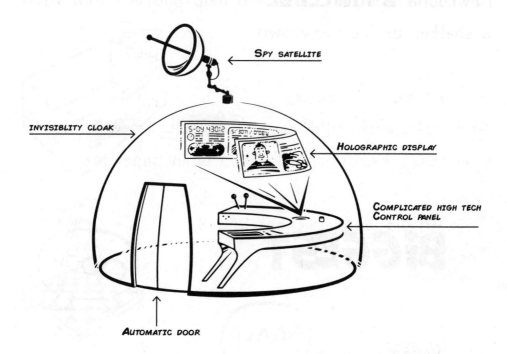

SPY SATELLITE

INVISIBLITY CLOAK

HOLOGRAPHIC DISPLAY

COMPLICATED HIGH TECH
CONTROL PANEL

AUTOMATIC DOOR

We had a look in our SECRET SHOEBOXES and
JAM JARS to see what **SUPER-COOL STUFF** we
had stashed away.

Now, what could be used to bring my **FANTASTIC** invention to life . . . ?

We came up with . . .

-   A spare shoebox

-   An old wooden chess board

-   A tea strainer

- A margarine tub

- Some paint

- Nails

- Sticky tape

Now, I know that there are a FEW bits and pieces missing **HERE AND THERE**, so it doesn't look EXACTLY like my original plan, but I'm still pretty pleased with it how it turned out . . .

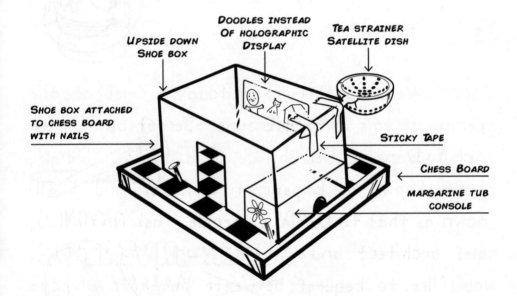

UPSIDE DOWN
SHOE BOX

DOODLES INSTEAD
OF HOLOGRAPHIC
DISPLAY

TEA STRAINER
SATELLITE DISH

SHOE BOX ATTACHED
TO CHESS BOARD
WITH NAILS

STICKY TAPE

CHESS BOARD

MARGARINE TUB
CONSOLE

# CLEVER, HUH?

I was excited to reveal the new **SUPER-SECRET SPY SHELTER** to Superdog.

I made a little speech and everything.

Would you like to hear it?

Yeah, I thought so:

Danny: We are gathered here today to celebrate the opening of this **AWESOME** Super-Secret Spy Shelter which I, Daniel . . . eurgh, "GARFIELD" . . . Dingle, better known as Experimental Face (and I AM known as that to LOADS of people – ask ANYONE!), chief architect and **SUPER-iNVENTOR**, would like to ~~bequeef~~ ~~bekweeth~~ ~~bekweath~~ give to Superdog, in honour of all that he has done in the name of psychic **GENIUS TOADS** everywhere.

But when we put the shelter down for Superdog to look at, he didn't seem as impressed by it as we'd thought he would be.

What he was impressed by, however, was the  puddle of mud next to it.

I guess that's understandable though.

**EVERYBODY** (even geniuses like Superdog and me) likes mud.

I have been *really excited* about Scout Camp
this week.

So excited, in fact, that I've hardly even noticed
that **SMUG, FULL-OF-HIMSELF, TWIT-FACED**
Gareth Trumpshaw has been even more of a twit
than usual.

He's just jealous that Percy and I beat him in the **Science Club Soap Box Derby** and knows that he can't be smug anymore.

(This doesn't mean that he doesn't still try.)

He is constantly rubbing it in our faces that his Dad works at **ACMETECH** and my Dad doesn't (not since he burnt half of it down anyway).

He also likes to ridicule me for having a toad as a pet. Superdog gets his own back though, by scorching his brains with **PSYCHIC LASER BEAMS** (at least, I assume that's what he's doing. If not, he's actually just glaring at him).

Luckily, smug, full-of-himself, twit-faced
Gareth Trumpshaw didn't join our Scout troop
(phew!).

He joined one on the other side of Greenville called
the 1st Eagles.

According to one of the older Scouts in our troop, the 1st Eagles used to be the only troop in Greenville, but when they kicked Scout Master Geoffrey out for trying to light a campfire **INDOORS**, he decided to form his own troop – the mighty **8TH EARTHWORMS!**

Gareth said that his Scout troop doesn't go on camping trips because they're "cold and rubbish and not super-cool at all".

Which is funny, because that's what all of the older Scouts said when we handed in our consent forms . . .

But what does Gareth know, anyway?

(Nothing – he's a **TWIT**.)

Debra Kirby (from the Roller Derby) is in a different Scout troop to us as well (the 4th Weasels), along with Nitty Neil (who has nits), Belinda (who hangs around with Nitty Neil too much and now also probably has nits), Michael and Leo (who have a lot of things wrong with them, but no nits).

In fact, it seems as though EVERYONE in Science Club has been conned into joining one Scout troop or another.

Anyway, the different Scout troops sometimes camped together, and I was REALLY hoping that Debra's would be going to this Scout camp too.

This is because:

- She **ALWAYS** shares her jelly squares

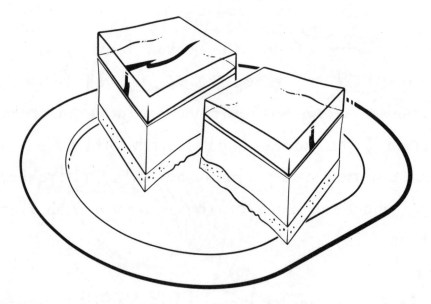

\-    She's FREAKISHLY STRONG and could help carry my backpack

This is definitely **NOT** because:

-    She's actually really nice and friendly

I mean, I don't **LIKE** her or anything like that – she's just handy to have around . . .

# I DON'T LIKE HER!

**Pfft,** what do you know anyway . . .

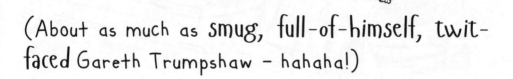

(About as much as smug, full-of-himself, twit-faced Gareth Trumpshaw – hahaha!)

Anyway, I asked Debra if she'd be going, but she said that she can't because her mum is driving in a rally at the weekend.

It turns out that Debra's mum is the famous professional lorry racer **DIESEL DORIS**!

I've never ever (EVER!) heard of her (I didn't even know that people raced lorries) but this somehow makes Debra **EVEN COOLER** as far as I'm concerned.

It also explains why Debra **LOVES** everything on wheels so much.

Debra said that I should come down to the track with her to watch her mum race sometime.

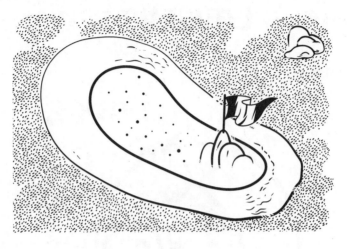

(I mean, she **TECHNICALLY** asked the whole class, but I knew she really just meant me.)

(Not that it matters, because I **DON'T** like her or anything, I like lorries . . .)

Anyway, I thought that this was an excellent idea. I was pretty sure that hanging out with lorry mechanics would be good for my **Spy Training.**

And N⊚T just because Debra Derby is lovely . . .

Wait, did I say **LOVELY?** I meant, erm . . .

GLOVELY!

Anyway,

We got into class and Miss Quimby told us all to

Miss Quimby **LOVES** doughnuts, and she can't live without having one at least once every half hour.

Which I totally understand, because doughnuts are DELICIOUS!

(Mmm, doughnuts . . .)

But she obviously hadn't had one in a while and I didn't want to get on her bad side today by doing anything like answering questions or working too hard, so I spent the morning doodling Debra driving a lorry.

Wait, did I say **DEBRA?** I meant, erm . . .

I was really pleased with my morning's doodling (**NOT** of Debra) until I looked over to see what Percy was doing, only to find that he'd copied my picture (**NOT** of Debra)!

ARGH!

Why do you **ALWAYS** have to copy me, Percy?

I told him that I had drawn Debra a zebra driving a lorry because I'd seen it on TV.

Then I had to **SCRIBBLE** all over my **EXCELLENT** doodle just to be sure that he did the same.

# PHEW!

I decided that I needed to just sit back and relax for a while after all this **STRESS** . . .

(Ah, lovely . . .)

. . . when I suddenly realised that I'd completely forgotten about PE class!

# SWEAT!

# ACHING LEGS!

# EXERCISE!

# NOOO!

I REALLY hope Ms Mills is in a good mood . . .

(Ms Mills is NEVER in a good mood.)

Ms Mills was NOT in a good mood.

She looked miserable and wanted us all to climb . . .

# THE ROPE!

Now, usually I would try and get out of something like this by talking to Ms Mills about Mr Hammond (she **LOVES** Mr Hammond), but she was looking particularly scary this morning (she'd probably just seen Mr Hammond talking to Miss Quimby again – that ALWAYS makes her mad) and I didn't want to risk being made to do army fitness drills (Ms Mills used to be in the army), so I decided to just get on with it.

I don't understand what the point of climbing 'The Rope' is (I don't think anyone does), so I tried to imagine a situation when knowing how to climb a rope might be useful.

Then it occurred to me that a rope might be hanging from Metal Face's **SUPER-SECRET SPY HELICOPTER** and that I will have to be able to climb it before the helicopter swoops off and saves me from **MORTAL DANGER!**

So I rushed to The Rope.

I started climbing up The Rope.

# OOF!

I fell off The Rope.

I gave up on The Rope.

Note to self: Make sure the spy helicopter has a ladder.

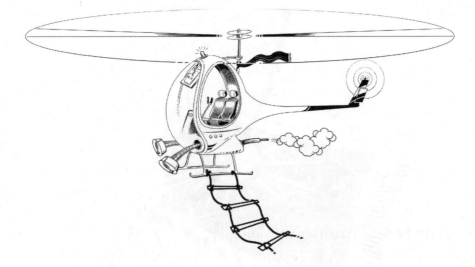

It seems like years and years and years and years and years have passed by, but finally . . .

**THE DAY FOR SCOUT CAMPING HAS ARRIVED!**

Hurray for Scout Camp! Hurray, Hurray!

That's **THREE WHOLE DAYS** camping in the wilds of . . .

**SUNNY SCOTLAND!**

I'm not absolutely sure where Scotland is, but I'm pretty sure that it's going to be **COOL** because it must be the only place in the ENTIRE WORLD where we would be allowed to try out all of this **SUPER-TOUGH SPY STUFF** (grr!):

-   How to use a compass

(GROWL!)

- How to navigate by the stars

(GRUNT!)

- How to tell the time from the sun

(SNARL!)

\-    How to identify edible plants

**(ROAR!)**

\-    How to pitch a tent

**(SNORT!)**

- How to start a fire (on purpose)

**(HOWL!)**

- How to put out a fire (also on purpose)

**(ERM . . . OINK?)**

Percy came over before the bus arrived to help me make sure that I'd packed **EVERYTHING** that I'd need.

I'd misplaced (lost) my packing list and Percy hadn't remembered to bring his (had lost his too), but I THINK that I've managed to pick up everything that I'll need to survive . . . **iN THE WiLD!**

- My super-secret, super-special inventor's kit

- My sleeping bag

- Sweets and crisps for midnight feast

\- Superdog

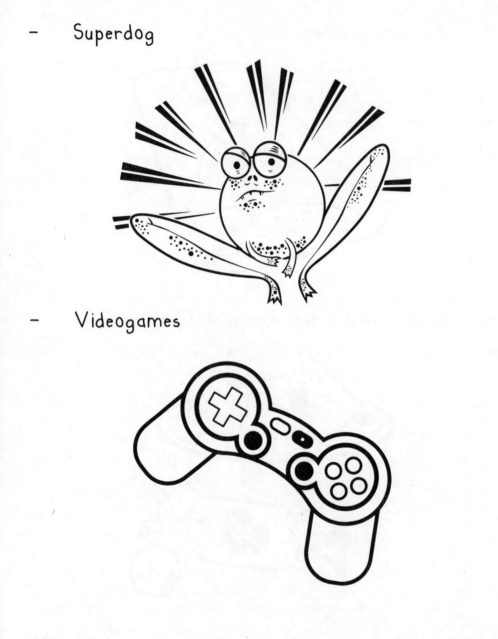

\- Videogames

\-     MP3 player

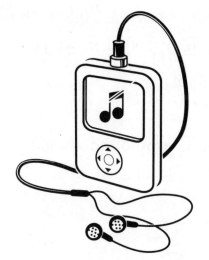

We'd even managed to talk Mum into letting us take some of Dad's new and extra-special **PICKLED EEL JELLY** with us!

Mum didn't WANT to let us take it, but I was so confident in my WORLD-RENOWNED PERSUASIVE SKILLS that I knew that I could seal the deal.

The techniques I employed include:

1) Bribery:

Danny: Can I take the jelly if I promise to only fart outdoors?

Mum: Oh no, I'm not falling for THAT ONE again. The neighbours were HORRIFIED when you poked your bottom out of the front door last week.

2) Repetition

## 3) ...Song?

Eventually I decided to try something completely new:

# TELLING THE TRUTH!

BUT ... MUUUM! PERCY AND I NEED TO TAKE THE JELLY. IF WE DON'T THEN WE'LL NEVER BE ABLE TO BECOME INCONTINENT LIKE METAL FACE!

SO YOU REALLY WANT TO BECOME INCONTINENT, DO YOU? WELL SUIT YOURSELVES THEN, TAKE THE JELLY ... BUT WHEN IT ALL GOES HORRIBLY WRONG, DON'T COME CRYING TO ME.

# RESULT!

Soon the bus arrived and Percy and I decided to sit at the back (because we are EASILY the oldest – and therefore the **COOLEST** – people here).

We couldn't wait until midnight to tuck into our snack food, so Percy and I decided to make a start on our crisps and sweets.

We were both sitting back, stuffed, when Percy started to go **GREEN**.

Oh no . . .

I quickly shouted out to the driver:

STOP THE BUS!
HE'S GONNA BLOW!

THERE ISN'T A REST STOP
FOR ANOTHER FIFTY MILES . . .
TELL HIM TO USE ONE OF THE
PAPER BAGS UNDER THE SEAT!

I tried to find a paper bag for Percy, but then
I remembered that we'd already wrecked our bags
by making **SUPER-FUNNY** hand puppets to
entertain Superdog.

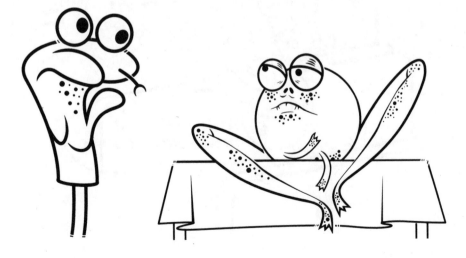

**PLEASE**, Percy, just fifty more miles — hold it together . . .

Percy pukes all over the back seat, me and Superdog.

# Why, Percy, why?

So now we're sat on the bus smelling of puke, and the bus driver is so **ANGRY** that Percy has been sick over the seats that he won't stop until we get to Scotland.

Superdog and I are not happy.

I have a sneaky feeling that the description we were given of 'Sunny Scotland' wasn't very accurate.

For instance, I haven't seen that much sun . . .

Actually, coming to think of it, I haven't seen ANY sun.

Actually, coming to think of it, I haven't seen any other Scout troops.

Actually, coming to think of it, we may not even be in Scotland, as I haven't seen any:

- Wild thistles

- Wild haggis

- Men in kilts (wild)

- Wild bagpipes

What I have seen, on the other hand, is:

-     Rain (coming down)

-     Rain (coming sideways)

-     Rain (doesn't stop coming)

Scout Master Geoffrey went and stood in the middle of what was **CLEARLY NOT A CAMP SITE** and asked us all whether we could remember if the bus driver had taken the second left onto the A902.

(I don't remember the bus driver taking anything except a dislike to me and Percy.)

Then he looked at his map to check that we've arrived at the right place.

(One of the Scouts had to point out that the map was uʍop ǝpᴉsdn.)

Another Scout then pointed to a barn and suggested that we were probably in a farmer's field.

Another scout just stood there, cold and covered in sick (this was me).

So we were getting soaked in a farmer's field with no idea where we were, and the bus with the angry bus driver had already driven off, complaining about kids being sick.

Hmm.

144

Fortunately, the barn in the field was unlocked, so we went and took shelter from the rain whilst Scout Master Geoffrey decided what to do.

He eventually decided not to call our parents and tell them to come and pick us up (phew!) but to pretend that we were on the REAL camp site, and that we would just carry on with our Scout Camp activities as usual.

This would usually have involved pitching our tents, but we had to wait for it to stop raining before we could go outside.

There wasn't really much to do in the barn, and almost all of the other Scouts had pulled out their videogames that they'd refused to leave at home. Scout Master Geoffrey wanted to make sure that we were doing something "Scouty", so he thought long and hard for a good forty-five minutes. Then he suggested that we play . . .

(You guessed it!)

YET ANOTHER game of rounders!

When it **FiNALLY** stopped raining (after nearly four hours and **HUNDREDS** of rounds of rounders – my legs!) it was dark outside.

We **STILL** hadn't pitched our tents.

Percy and I hadn't packed a torch like the other Scouts, but we decided to go and find somewhere in the dark where the ground was really soft so it would be easier to knock the tent pegs into the ground.

Clever, huh?

After about half an hour of playing around in the mud (**FUN**) and walking into fence posts (**NOT FUN**), we were pretty sure that we'd found a really great spot and put up our tent.

Percy then pointed out that if it had been raining **ALL DAY**, surely pretty much all of the ground would have been soft enough.

Why, Percy, WHY?

So after playing around in the mud a bit more (STiLL **FUN**) and hammering everything in sight with our tent peg mallets (including ourselves and each other — 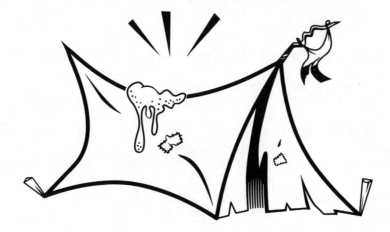ouch!), we decided that our tent was probably good enough and went back to the barn.

**F!**

Stupid fence posts.

It was getting close to dinner time, and everybody was getting **HUNGRY**.

The idea had been to heat up some baked beans and sausages on the camp fire.

Unfortunately, it had started raining again (**SURPRISE, SURPRISE!**) and nobody trusted Scout Master Geoffrey's abilities to make a fire indoors without **KILLING US ALL** (we'd all heard the story about his experience in the 1st Eagles by then), so Scout Master Geoffrey had to improvise by heating up everyone's food on a Bunsen burner.

No one had **ANY** idea why Scout Master Geoffrey had a Bunsen burner (maybe he **IS** a super-secret spy after all . . .), but it quickly became obvious that it was going to take all night to cook, so we all decided just to leave him to it.

We tried to ignore our hunger by playing videogames and stuffing hay down each other's uniforms, but we couldn't stop thinking about **FOOD** and regretted having eaten our midnight snacks on the bus.

Rob Plant had started licking his hand, trying to get as much of the taste of his crisps from it as possible.

James Paige started to look at his own arm in a really worrying "that looks tasty" way.

Even Superdog was eyeing up a particularly **DEAD-LOOKING** mouse.

Then I suddenly remembered – Dad's jelly!

RESULT!

I handed it around and everyone stuffed it in their mouths.

It only took a couple of minutes for the **AWESOME POWER** of the jelly to take effect.

First, Jonathan Bonham complained that it made his mouth feel funny.

Then Paul Jones said that his stomach was gurgling.

Then Percy looked at Superdog licking the dead mouse, and was sick.

Typical.

This combination of jelly and seeing Percy barfing set off a chain reaction, and soon all of the Scouts were being sick.

That is, except for me.

There wasn't enough jelly for me after I'd passed it around, and Mum always said I should offer everyone else things first.

Thanks, Mum!

It was really starting to smell in our part of the barn, so I decided to go over to Scout Master Geoffrey and inform him of the sick situation.

There was a lot of black smoke coming out of the bottom of the tiny saucepan Scout Master Geoffrey was using to cook the beans with, but the mashed-up sausage mess that had risen to the top of the pile still looked raw.

Needless to say, I didn't have high hopes for dinner.

Scout Master Geoffrey eventually gave up on the beans and went to clean up the puke and help everyone who was feeling ILL.

I, on the other hand, managed to pick out a bit of sausage that wasn't too raw or too burnt, and it didn't actually taste all that bad, so I decided to just help myself.

No one else seemed to be that hungry anymore, so I was sure that they wouldn't mind.

By the time everyone had stopped being sick it was time for bed, so Percy and I made our way to our tent.

After another half hour of stumbling through the rain and walking into **MORE FENCE POSTS**, we managed to find our tent and settled down for a good night's sleep.

Only, it **WASN'T** a good night's sleep.

This was mostly because our "**GREAT PLACE**" to set up our tent was actually right by the bank of the river.

In fact, there was so much water that it had pulled the tent pegs up out of the ground, so when Percy finally woke up and walked into the main pole (OOF!), the tent collapsed on us.

Percy, Superdog and I only just managed to find the entrance and scramble our way out before our tent took off with all our stuff, whirling down the river and only stopping when it got stuck in some reeds...

We were sad about our tent (especially Superdog – I think he was quite enjoying all the water) but we knew that Scout Master Geoffrey wouldn't mind if we shared his tent with him, so we decided to splosh our way over to his pitch.

SPLISH!

SPLOSH!

SPLISH!

OOF! (Why, fence post, WHY?)

It later turned out that Scout Master Geoffrey
wasn't a big fan of sharing his tent.

Or of talking about how cool Metal Face is.

Or of being stared at by Superdog.

Or farting.

When he finally cracked and started shouting at us, I tried to explain that we HAD to keep farting if we wanted to become incontinent.

He then said something about giving us something to wet ourselves about (I don't think he knew what "incontinent" meant) . . .

It turned out that he ACTUALLY meant . . .

# POTATO PEELING!

Scout Master Geoffrey told us that our packing list said **NO PETS** were allowed at Scout Camp.

I was going to argue that Superdog wasn't just a "pet", but I didn't want to reveal his **SECRET IDENTITY**. So Percy and I were put on potato peeling duty **ALL MORNING**.

It was pretty boring once we'd finished throwir potatoes at each other and actually had to them, but somehow we knew that it was than what the other Scouts are doing.

Scout Master Geoffrey had decided that as he only had a few bundles of rope with him that the Scouts should try to earn their Knotting Badges.

I'm not sure whether this is a real badge or not (or why Scout Master Geoffrey is so **OBSESSED** with knotting **EVERYTHING**), but they had to spend all morning tying and untying different knots in rope.

(At least they didn't have to climb them . . . leurgh!)

Everyone came back to the barn for lunch, but there was no way of cooking the potatoes that we'd been peeling (I assume that was the point) as it was STILL raining and the gas had run out on the Bunsen burner.

So the afternoon's activity got changed to potato carving.

Scout Master Geoffrey told us to try to carve our potato into the shape of something, and if it was a good enough likeness then we would earn a Potato Carving Badge (this is **DEFINITELY** not a real badge).

The other Scouts obviously weren't convinced by this either, so they didn't actually TOUCH their potatoes.

When Scout Master Geoffrey asked them what they had made, they just said stuff like:

-    Asteroids

-    Flat footballs

-    Frightened, bald hedgehogs

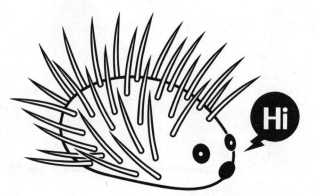

(This was a clever idea – wish Percy and I had thought of it.)

By the time Percy and I had finished **HACKING OUR POTATOES TO BITS**, they didn't really look like anything, so we just decided to say:

## "CHIPS!"

As the evening rolled around, it was **STILL** raining.

We were supposed to have had a bonfire and "a sing-song", but the campfire was obviously cancelled.

So Scout Master Geoffrey improvised and brought out a bag of marshmallows for us to toast one at a time over his matches.

Then he told us to sing one of the campfire songs that we'd learnt at Scouts last week.

No one could remember any of the songs (because they were **RUBBISH**) so we all just guessed at a style and started to sing whatever we knew.

Scout Master Geoffrey couldn't think of anything else for us to do after our sing-song (we had all refused to play **ANY MORE ROUNDERS**), so he just left us to throw our potato masterpieces at each other in peace.

At the end of the evening, when we were all sporting potato wounds and covered in potato-shaped bruises, Scout Master Geoffrey decided to tell us about the **AWESOME RAFT CHALLENGE** that would be held at Swan Lake Park.

He said that we would have to build our own raft and race it against the ones built by other Scouts.

He also said that there would be lots of different Scout troops participating and that there would be a special prize for the best raft.

Scouts were supposed to be divided into teams of four for the challenge, but as there were only six of us, Percy and I were given a team of our own (also, no one wanted to go with us after the eel jelly incident . . .)

I think that this is a better arrangement. I don't want all of the other Scouts finding out about our top-secret laboratory . . . I mean, top-secret **CLUBHOUSE!**

Percy and I went off to sleep in Scout Master Geoffrey's tent (he'd decided to sleep in the barn), talking about how we were going to make our raft the **COOLEST RAFT EVER!**

But, as Scout Master Geoffrey had the best tent, we decided that it would be unfair to let all of the other Scouts spend another night in their rubbishly-constructed tents, so we invited them all over to tell horror stories and fart all night.

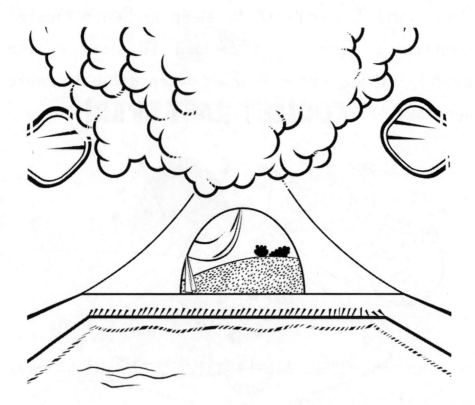

It got a bit **HOT AND SMELLY** in there after a while, so we decided to do Scout Master Geoffrey a massive favour and cut a few ventilation holes in his tent.

He can thank us for it later — he could have suffocated in there!

On reflection, I'm not sure how useful Scout Camp has been for my **SPY TRAINING.**

What we were supposed to learn:

- How to use a compass

- How to navigate by the stars

- How to start a fire

- How to put out a fire

- How to tell time from the sun

- How to identify edible plants

- How to pitch a tent

What we **ACTUALLY** learnt:

- **NEVER** let Scout Master Geoffrey organise **ANYTHING**

- **NEVER** let Percy decide where to pitch your tent

- Fence posts are **NOT** your friends

- A potato doesn't really look like anything other than a **POTATO**

- **NEVER** stand/sit/exist within vomiting range of Percy (bleurgh!)

- Scout Camp is **RUBBISH**

- Dad's jelly-making skills are **AWESOME!**

The other Scouts had to pack up their tents before we left, but as Percy and I didn't have to pack anything (except Superdog) because it was all floating down the river somewhere, we spent the morning looking for COOL STUFF to take back to our secret lab – I mean, CLUBHOUSE!

We didn't find too much COOL stuff though – just sticks and rocks, mainly.

However, Superdog did manage to find a **HUGE** wriggling beetle, so at least Superdog got to have a snack.

Percy sees Superdog chewing on the dung beetle and is **SICK** . . . on my shoes.

Why, Percy, **WHY?**

He had a whole field to be sick in!

I've just heard the **WORST NEWS EVER!**

It turns out that **smug, full-of-himself, twit-faced** Gareth Trumpshaw is going to enter the raft challenge too!

His Scout troop weren't even going to take part!

He just wants to get **revenge** on us for winning the Derby last term.

So, as usual, he'll be entering the challenge on his own.

He thinks he's SO superior . . .

He isn't.

He's a **twit**.

I spent all day in school doodling pictures of Gareth Trumpshaw looking like a twit, being a twit and acting like a twit.

This is easy.

I just draw Gareth Trumpshaw – hahaha!

Then Debra Derby skated over to see what I was doing, so I told her about the raft challenge.

Debra then said that her troop was doing the raft challenge too and that she had already had lots of great ideas.

She didn't actually tell me her ideas, but her friend Amy Almond is a welder and together they probably know a lot about mechanics.

Their team could be fierce competition in the raft race, but that doesn't really matter because her Scout troop is probably a normal one, not a super-cool super-spy training Scout troop like mine (or so I've told everyone else).

I got home from school and decided to leave my homework for later as it was time I got on with the **ALL-IMPORTANT TASK** of making improvements to Superdog's shelter.

I had learnt my lesson from the tent peg DISASTER at camp and was busy banging in as many nails into it as I could when Dad came up to the clubhouse with Grandad Leonard.

He and Granny Jean had stopped by as they were on their way to something called a "Sci-Fi Convention".

Dad says it's a place where lots of geeks dress up like people from old sci-fi TV programmes and pretend that they have exciting lives.

He sounds as though this was a HARROWING experience for him growing up.

Granny Jean and Grandad Leonard are completely mad about sci-fi (more like **"SIGH"**-fi, hahaha!), and they love this old series called **"STAR TRIP"**, so they're always travelling around going to conventions and things.

This is okay though. I know that Dad must surely get his inventing skills from Grandad Leonard's love of finding new ways to prevent an alien attack, so I guess it's all worked out quite well for me in the end.

Grandad wanted to show Dad and me a new **"PHASER"** that he'd made.

It didn't do anything except light up and make a noise, but it was pretty cool all the same.

PEW PEW...

I tell Dad and Grandad Leonard about the raft race challenge and how there's going to be a special prize.

I also tell them how Gareth Trumpshaw will probably win (because he's smug, full-of-himself and twit-faced).

(Oh, and his dad works at **ACMETECH!**)

This makes my dad quite angry, because he doesn't like Gareth Trumpshaw's dad almost as much as (probably more than) I don't like Gareth Trumpshaw.

My dad thinks that Gareth's Trumpshaw's dad was responsible for making him lose his job at AcmeTech . . . This is a bit suspicious. Gareth Trumpshaw's dad was actually nowhere near the AcmeTech factory when my dad accidentally set it on fire.

I am happy to overlook this fact so that I can have Dad's help beating Gareth and his dad, Twit-face senior.

I also tell Dad and Grandad how Debra Derby is entering too, and that Debra's mum is Diesel Doris, the famous lorry racer.

Grandad says:

**GD**: Really? She's lovely. Good, strong legs . . .

We all look at each other awkwardly. **WHY** is Grandad looking at Diesel Doris' legs? **WHY** is he telling us that he has been looking at Diesel Doris' legs?

Percy doesn't puke (for once).

Well done, Percy.

Dad and Grandad decided that we should join forces to build the raft to annoy Gareth Trumpshaw, humiliate Gareth Trumpshaw's dad and win the admiration of Debra Derby's mum, Diesel Doris (and, apparently, her legs).

With three generations of  GENIUS inventors (and Superdog . . . and Percy, I suppose) our raft is bound to be INVINCIBLE!

Dad says the raft should be ~~submergat~~ ~~submermal~~ ~~sub~~ able to go under water, like a submarine.

Grandad suggests that it should also be able to travel at **LIGHT SPEED**, like a space ship.

I think both of these ideas are great, but I'd be content with the raft just not sinking . . . like a raft.

We've been working on the raft for a few days now.

Dad and Grandad have invaded the clubhouse for their "secret meetings" . . .

. . . but actually Mum has decided that they're not allowed in the house whilst they are helping me with my raft.

This is because:

-    Grandad "borrowed" her microwave oven to create a teleportation machine

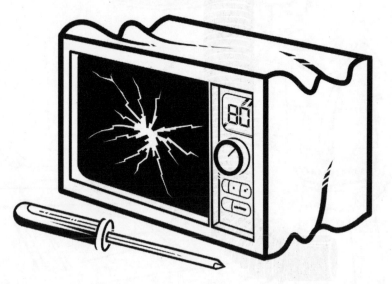

\-     Dad "borrowed" the vacuum cleaner pipe to try and make a periscope by bending the pipe and jamming some binoculars into the brush.

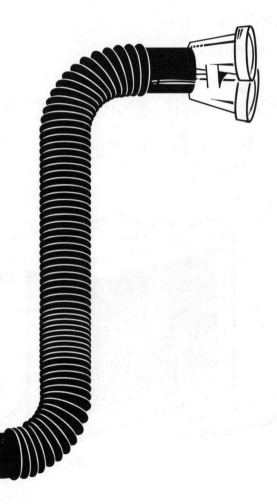

Dad and Grandad are really enthusiastic about the raft, and they keep talking about where the propellers are going to go and where to put the oxygen supply . . .

Thanks to this, Percy and I can focus on decorating the raft and making it cool enough for Metal Face to be so proud of us that he just HAS to employ us.

On Saturday morning, Percy and I leave Dad and Grandad inventing in the clubhouse whilst we make our way to our Scout Meeting.

I secretly hope that no one in the Scout Troop will notice the latest MASSIVE DISASTER:

My Scout (spy) uniform has just come out of the wash and it's turned black!

This is **entirely** Granny Jean's fault, because she tried to wash her Sci-Fi costume with all of our laundry.

Percy says the uniform is cool and that it makes me "look more like a spy".

Scout Master Geoffrey **DOESN'T** agree.

When he sees my uniform he assumes that I've dyed it black on purpose (he must have overheard our IncontiNinja talk in the tent at Scout camp) and puts me on potato peeling duty.

Percy laughs at me, so he gets put on potato peeling duty too – **hahaha!**

I don't know why we have to peel potatoes — the Scouts have all eaten already.

Also, why does Scout Master Geoffrey always have such a big supply of potatoes that need peeling?

What does he use them for?

We ask all the other Scouts how their rafts are coming along, but they all just laughed and said:

Scouts: You aren't actually **GOING** to the raft race, are you?

I am now more determined than ever, and get home to find Grandad Leonard and Dad in the clubhouse fighting over the design of the suit that they want me to wear.

Grandad Leonard has decided to make me a space suit, although I'm not convinced that the suit would actually keep me alive in outer space as it seems to be made mostly out of:

Bin liners

. . . and duct tape

He has to tape me into it and cut me out of it . . .

Hmm . . .

The helmet is an old upside down fishbowl.

It would look pretty good, but there's **no way** of getting it over my head.

After about half an hour of trying to get the fish bowl over my ears, Grandad finally realises that if he **DID** manage to get the fishbowl on my head, we'd never be able to get it off again and I'd have to eat all my meals through a straw.

I decide to put Grandad Leonard's idea on the back burner.

Dad, on the other hand, has made me a scuba diving suit out of:

Bin liners

. . . and duct tape

I'm seeing a pattern emerge.

I look over to Superdog for help, but he hasn't got any idea how to make them stop either.

The scuba goggles are made out of a margarine tub, cling film and a rubber band.

I feel that this was a noble attempt at using some of our C☺☺L **FINDS.** I didn't tell Dad that the margarine box was too big for my face and would never keep any water out of my eyes.

Percy and I decide that it's time to get **SERIOUS.** The raft race is in **ONE WEEK.**

We get out the instruction sheet that Scout Master Geoffrey gave us and have a look to see what bits we're missing.

We're supposed to have:

# KEY COMPONENTS:

-     A wooden base

-     Something to make the raft float (barrels, polystyrene, etc)

- Rope to hold it all together

- Paddles

## OPTIONAL ITEMS:

- Decoration

- Homemade propulsion system

## FORBIDDEN ITEMS:

- Outboard motors

- Actual boats, dinghys, canoes

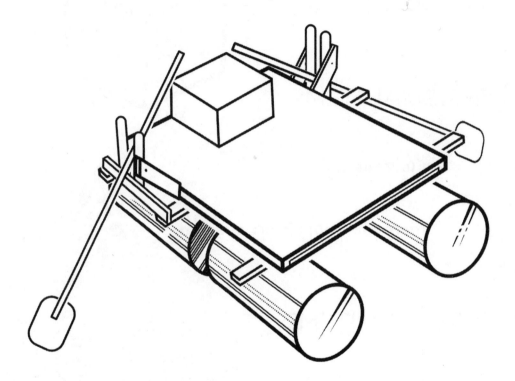

What we actually have is:

- Cardboard

- Christmas lights

- Phasers

- A periscope

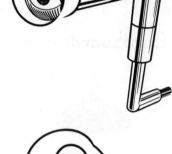

- A stuffed parrot

I decide to call a **SUPER-SECRET EMERGENCY MEETING** of our highly qualified design team and we all get to work.

We realise that we don't really have a frame for the raft, or anything to stop the frame from sinking, or anything to hold those bits together...

Dad and Grandad Leonard rush around all day, finding all these important missing pieces.

Percy and I are still focused on decoration and cover EVERYTHING IN SIGHT with tin foil.

Superdog gets friendly with the stuffed parrot (I'm sure there is some kind of secret spy toad-parrot code that us mere humans don't know about. So I trust he is doing a good job).

It takes all day, but we finally manage it . . .

We step back to look at our work.

This is the initial design . . .

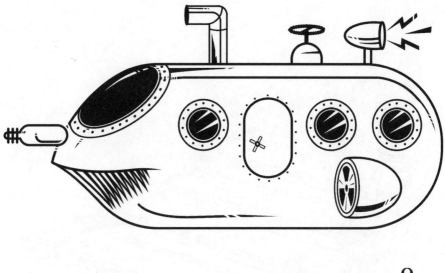

This is the final result . . .

# BEHOLD the **SUPER-SONIC SUBMARINE!**

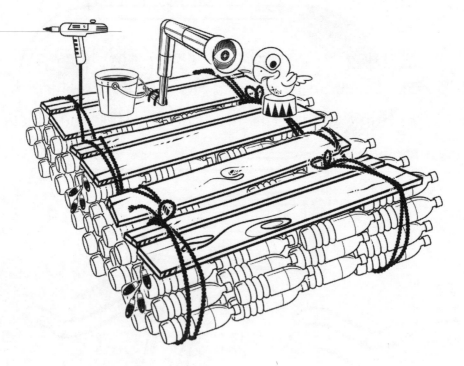

Grandad says that we'll need some ammo for the **ENEMIES.**

I'm not sure what **ENEMIES** he's talking about.

Anyway...

He's thinking of something along the lines of a deflector shield and ray guns (he's **ALWAYS** thinking of something along the lines of a deflector shield and ray guns).

Dad was thinking of something along the lines of **heat-seeking missiles.**

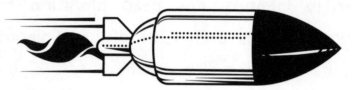

We hunt around the house, shed, garage and garden.

The closest we manage to get is a bucket of soot.

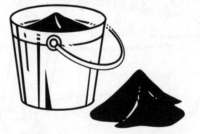

Mum comes to remind us to not get **TOO MESSY** as we have Granny Jean's garden tea party after the raft race.

Apparently Granny has been planning the tea party for months and a lot of her friends from the Sci-Fi society will be there.

She's invited the vicar, the mayor and some famous actors that I've never heard of from an old TV series about life in outer space.

Almost ALL of these people AREN'T going to be there, but Grandma wants to make a really good impression, just in case, so it's important that we arrive on time and looking smart.

I tell Mum not to worry!

**FINALLY,** the big day arrives.

Dad and Grandad Leonard spend the best part of the morning taping Percy and me into our bin liner spaceman–scuba suits.

We feel **RIDICULOUS**.

We look **RIDICULOUS**.

But I give Percy the C☺☺L STUFF Collector's Neck Pouch to wear for good luck, so at least I don't look quite as **RIDICULOUS** as he does.

I've also spent a lot of time making Superdog a tin foil captain's hat. He is, after all, the true GENIUS behind all of this.

I'm sure he and the stuffed parrot have worked out some kind of ~~super-secret~~ plan to guarantee our victory.

Dad, Grandad and Superdog then load the **Super-Sonic Submarine** onto the roof of Grandad's car and we make our way towards Swan Lake Park.

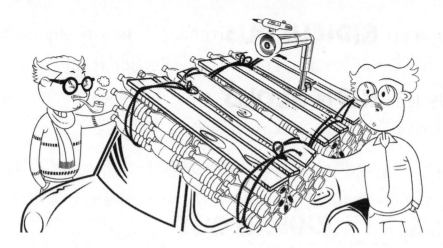

They park the car at the top of a hill and we slide the raft down towards the lake.

On arriving we see that although this was supposed to be a raft race for all of the Scout groups in Greenville, it seems that only the kids from the Science Club are taking part.

–　　Debra Derby and Amy Almond have used big tyre inner tubes for their raft . . . and they've remembered to bring paddles! (I knew we'd forgotten something!) They've also brought ammunition . . . a big bucket of used motor oil!

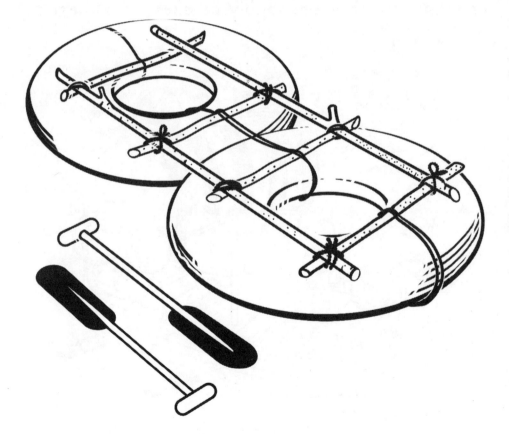

-    Nitty Neil (who has **NITS**) and Belinda (who probably now has **NITS** as well) have created a very impressive raft that looks a lot like a Viking ship. It has hand crafted paddles and a sail and everything. I'm not sure if they've brought ammunition, it will probably be axes, or something else Viking-y!

—   Leo and Michael have brought a pretty standard raft . . . but it's their weapons I'm worried about: They have a bucket of flour, a bucket of eggs and a bucket of what looks like lard.

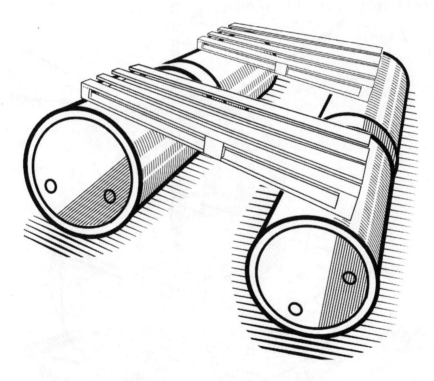

\-  As for Gareth's raft . . . It's made out the frame of a dispensing machine, turned on its side with all sorts of fancy floats. It also has rotating paddles and a shield system . . . why didn't we think of that?

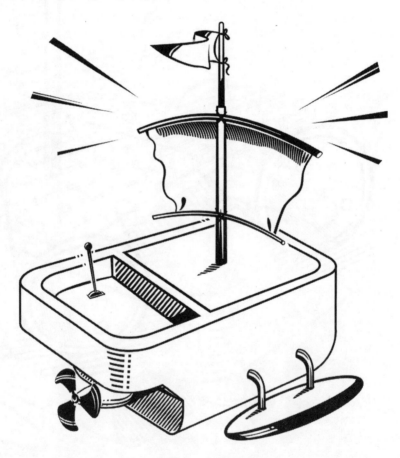

His Dad is walking around the raft with a screwdriver and a blow torch making final adjustments.

He spots my dad and waves politely. My dad, very maturely (**NOT!**) smiles (**STICKS HIS TONGUE OUT**) at him . . . he's **SO EMBARASSING!**

The competition judges examine all the rafts and then they announce:

"After some deliberation and for the sake of safety we've decided not to hold the competition in the lake. We'll hold the race in the duck pond as it's much shallower and less dangerous."

We all look over at the ducks and they look back at us, unconvinced.

We drag our rafts over to the edge of the duck pond.

**NOW**

ALL YOU HAVE TO DO IS SAIL YOUR RAFT FROM ONE END OF THE POND TO THE OTHER AND BACK AGAIN. THE WINNER WILL BE THE FIRST RAFT TO GET BACK TO THIS SIDE.

WE DON'T WANT ANY CONFRONTATIONS . . . NO PUSHING EACH OTHER OFF, NO THROWING THINGS AT EACH OTHER! . . . WE WANT A GOOD, CLEAN RACE.

We all look across the duck pond; it's no more than a hundred meters to the other end and back . . . piece of cake, right?

When we get the signal we all push our rafts into the water and get on.

Our Super-Sonic Submarine does not quite do what Dad promised. It definitely isn't **SUPER** or **SONiC**, but it is a submarine.

We start to sink pretty quickly.

SWISH...

Percy uses Superdog's **GENIUS** tin foil pirate hat to throw all the water back into the pond.

Debra Derby and Amy Almond start paddling their raft towards the other side of the pond; as does Gareth Trumpshaw.

Percy and I didn't remember to bring paddles —
just the Christmas lights, the periscope and the
stuffed parrot.

None of these things are really helping much, so
our raft just drifts to the middle of the pond.

Even from this far away I can see the arrogant look on smug, full-of-himself, twit-faced Gareth Trumpshaw's face.

Leo and Michael aren't doing too well either though, their raft has inched towards us very slowly, but is now sinking. They give up on attempting to win the race and instead bombard the opposition with flour and eggs.

The Viking ship is really impressive, but maybe a bit **TOO IMPRESSIVE?**

Everything seems OK at first as Neil and Belinda paddle the ship towards the other end of the duck pond, but as the wind picks up they run into problems.

It's quite dramatic; at first I think it's heading for Debra and Amy, but a final gust of wind blows them into Gareth's raft.

Nitty Neil and Belinda take their chance and start throwing lard into Gareth's vessel. It does the job, after a few more eggs and half a bucket of flour, it looks more like a floating cake than a raft.

Nice one, Nitty Neil and Belinda.

CRACK...

Gareth decides to jump onto the Viking ship. He just makes it when he's hit by a big dollop of flying lard.

This is hilarious. Gareth grabs what looks like a water balloon from the Viking ship and throws it at Neil and Belinda. It misses them and hits Percy. The balloon EXPLODES. It is full of DOG SICK.

Percy goes green and **PUKES** in our bucket of soot . . .

Why, Percy, why?

At this point I realise that the wind has changed and the Viking ship is heading towards us on a **COLLISION COURSE**. Percy and I are completely doomed; our raft is just drifting around in the middle of the pond.

Percy and I decide we'd better start paddling with our legs...

As we paddle, I start to realise we're passing parts of our raft as they fall off and float away.

If I hadn't spent all day at Scout camp peeling potatoes while the Scouts were all learning to tie knots, this probably wouldn't be happening.

Percy starts to **PANiC** and he accidentally kicks the bucket on our raft through the air; it lands right next to Dad and Grandad, covering them both in **PUKE** and **SOOT**.

At this point, Percy and I have accepted that we're probably not going to win this race. That is unless somebody can throw us some sticky tape and waterproof items we could use to make a new raft.

Or just a whole new raft.

This seems **unLikeLy.**

It seems even more unlikely when Debra and Amy's raft passes us. They've already made it to the other side of the duck pond and are heading back to claim their victory.

Percy and I try to grab onto their raft, mainly for a lift back to dry land, but Amy Almond throws motor oil over us so that we slip and slide and Percy, who valiantly got one leg on the side of the raft, slips straight back off and splashes Superdog and me with a combination of pond water, lard and oil.

Everyone seems to have lost interest in the race now as **ALL-OUT WAR** has broken out.

A few parents and Scout Master Geoffrey rush over to fish people out of the pond.

Scout Master Geoffrey is the first to receive a balloon of **DOG SICK** to the face, followed shortly after by half a bucket of flour.

The more people who try to help, the worse it gets.

Gareth Trumpshaw, smug as ever, stands on top of the Viking ship (which is also starting to sink) waving his arms and shouting that it's **'SO UNFAIR'**.

Belinda quickly shuts him up with a **DOG SICK** balloon in the face.

Percy and I decide to wade over to the other side of the pond where Debra Derby and Amy Almond are waiting for their prize.

Eventually everyone gathers the bits of raft out of the pond and we all get together to congratulate Debra and Amy.

Nobody hangs around for very long though, the smell of **FISH GUTS, EGGS, PUKE** and **LARD** is

 DISGUSTING

It's not long before Percy is sick, on his own shoes.

**TYPICAL.**

Scout Master Geoffrey announces that Debra and Amy have won . . . a **WEEK'S CAMPING TRIP IN SUNNY SCOTLAND!**

They seem really happy. Smug, full of himself, twit-faced Gareth Trumpshaw looks really disappointed and his Dad starts shouting that the Viking ship should be disqualified.

Percy and I are both really pleased we didn't win. We're also really pleased that Gareth Trumpshaw is so upset that he didn't win.

We all head back towards the cars with bits of our rafts. When Dad, Grandad, Percy and I get to the top of the hill we notice that the car has gone **MISSING**.

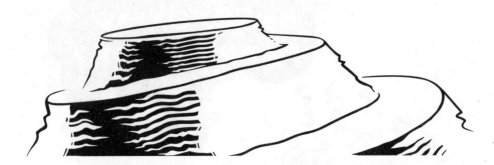

DAD: "Oh no! Someone's stolen the car!"

Suddenly we hear a **DESPERATE SCREAM** from the bottom of the hill. It's Scout Master Geoffrey.

It looks like Grandad forgot to leave the handbrake on and his car rolled down the hill and

into Scout Master Geoffrey's mobile fish and chip van.

Finally, I discover what he uses all those potatoes for!

Dad and Grandad go and sort out insurance papers; by this time we're starting to run late for Granny Jean's tea party. There's no time for Dad to sneak home and change, and the car has to be towed.

Fortunately, Debra Derby and her mum, Diesel Doris, pull up to see if we're all okay. They offer to give us a lift to Granny's tea party in her classic, open-backed American army truck.

Dad and Grandad have to sit in the back of the truck as they're covered from head to toe in a **REVOLTING, EGGY-PUKY-SOOTY-FISH-GUTTY MUSH.**

Amy Almond and Debra Derby help to cut Percy and I out of our bin liner duct tape scuba suits.

Thanks to these, we've managed to stay completely dry and clean.

Unlike Dad and Grandad. . .

We're allowed to sit in the front of the truck with Superdog (who has managed to keep his captain's hat on!).

It had been quite a peaceful afternoon on Crescent Hill as some of the elderly members of the local Sci-Fi society had enjoyed a *quiet garden* tea party.

Suddenly there was a **THUNDEROUS ROAR** and the street started to shake.

Neighbours came out of their houses to see what was happening as an army truck pulled up outside number sixty-two. One old lady lost her false teeth during the chaos.

Quite a few gnomes also lost their balance because of the rumble.

All of the guests at Granny's tea party **RUSH OUT** to the front garden. They are faced with a huge army truck parked across Granny Jean's petunias.

"I KNEW IT" shouts a neighbour.

**"IT'S PART OF THE CONSPiRACY - THEY'VE COME TO SiLENCE US!"**

**"NO!"** says another.

"They've been planning an alien invasion! Have you seen how they dress?"

All of Granny's guests (who are in full costume) start to **panic** and ***RUSH AROUND***, tripping over shell-shocked gnomes and trampling on Granny Jean's flower bed.

Seeing all the guests **panic** makes the neighbours **panic**, and they soon surround the house throwing eggs and rotten fruit.

SHMM...

Granny's guests retaliate by pointing STUN GUNS and phasers at the neighbours. They don't do much though, besides light up and make cool noises.

Dad and Grandad Leonard get out of the back of the van to try to calm things down. Suddenly, everyone stops and takes a step back.

The smell is so **OVERPOWERING** that people start being sick on the street.

Percy starts to go green. I do what any GENIUS would do in this situation.

I open my door and throw him out, just in time for him to puke over the old lady's false teeth.

Why, Percy, **WHY?**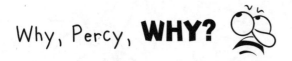

Eventually Mum comes to the rescue with a hose pipe. She hoses down Dad and Grandad Leonard, the house, the false teeth and any neighbours that are making a fuss.

Nice one, Mum.

Granny Jean goes indoors to get Dad and Grandad a towel and a change of clothes, then banishes them to the shed.

Eventually Debra and her mum leave and normality is resumed on Crescent Hill, aside from the fact that Granny Jean's garden has been completely trashed.

Percy and I lie low in the kitchen whilst all the guests leave.

Although they do tell Granny Jean it was by far the **BEST** tea party they've ever been to!

Mum wants to know how we did in the raft race. I tell her we didn't win. She's **REALLY IMPRESSED** that Percy and I have managed to stay so clean though, especially seeing as Dad and Grandad arrived home in such a mess.

Granny Jean eventually lets Dad and Grandad out of the shed; just in time to watch a tow-truck pull up outside the front of the house with Grandad's mangled car on the back.

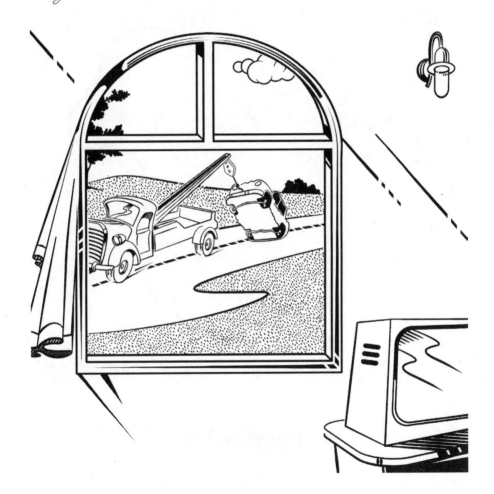

Granny Jean **DOESN'T LOOK HAPPY.** She turns
to shout at Dad and Grandad, but they've already
locked themselves back in the shed.

Mum then announces:

MUM: Boys, I think you've done really well for managing to stay clean and for obviously being a lot more sensible and responsible than Dad and Grandad; I think you deserve a special treat.

# RESULT!

I **DO** deserve a special treat!

Percy and Superdog probably don't, but I wouldn't be a very good spy if I turned my back on my sidekicks, would I?

# What could it be...? Another visit to METALWAY...?

A new bike?

I CAN SEE THAT SINCE YOU WENT TO SCOUT CAMP YOU'VE BOTH BECOME REALLY RESPONSIBLE. I'VE SPOKEN TO PERCY'S PARENTS AND WE'VE DECIDED TO SEND YOU BOTH ON ANOTHER CAMPING TRIP TO SUNNY SCOTLAND. THIS TIME YOU'LL BE AWAY FOR TWO WHOLE WEEKS!

Percy and I both look at each other thinking the same thing: **IT WAS GOING TO BE THE LONGEST TWO WEEKS OF OUR LIVES.**

We look out of the front window. Superdog is sitting on the lawn in the front garden eating a pile of **FISH GUTS**.

Percy pukes.

I know, Percy, I know.

Now it's **YOUR TURN.** This is my present to you. (Aren't I kind?)

**DANNY DINGLE** presents . . .

# YOUR VERY OWN SUPER-SECRET SPY NOTEBOOK!!

## TA-DA!

This will help you become a **SUPERHERO AND SUPER-SECRET SPY** like me. Because I think we all know that super-secret spies are **awesome**.

# MISSION #1

Every superhero needs a nemesis. Use mine until you find one of your own! This is smug, full-of-himself, twit-faced Gareth Trumpshaw's **TWIT FACE**. Your mission: make him look as twittish as possible. Grab a pen and go **WILD!**

# MISSION #2

To be a **TRUE SUPERHERO**, you need a cool way to get around. I have the **Metal-Mobile** and the **Super-Sonic Submarine**, but you can't copy me (unless you want to be a sidekick like Percy).

What would your super-cool method of transport be?

Where will you go first?

# MISSION #3

This is the most exciting bit! THIS is where your idea becomes real!
Go on a quest around your house and find things to make your
vehicle out of. Use this space to draw your plans:

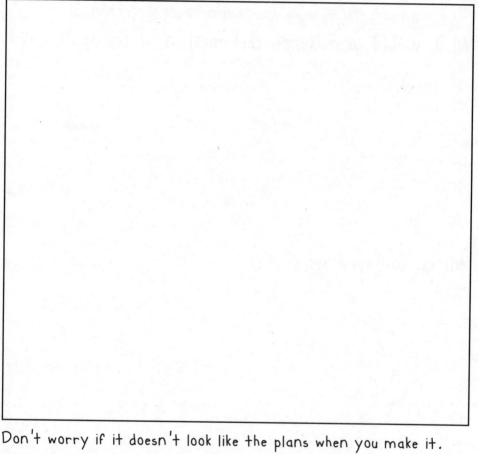

Don't worry if it doesn't look like the plans when you make it.
I mean, just look at how the Super-sonic submarine turned out!
(Still awesome.)

# MISSION #4

Now it's time to take the offensive. Go back to your improved version of Gareth Trumpshaw (what a **TWIT!**) and rip it out. If someone asks you why you're ripping pages out of a book, you can tell them you're improving your **super-secret spy skills!**

Next, rip this page out too. On the back, you'll find a guide that will help you make the ⓑⒺⓈⓉ paper airplane ⒺⓋⒺⓇ!

Use Gareth Trumpshaw's face for target practice.

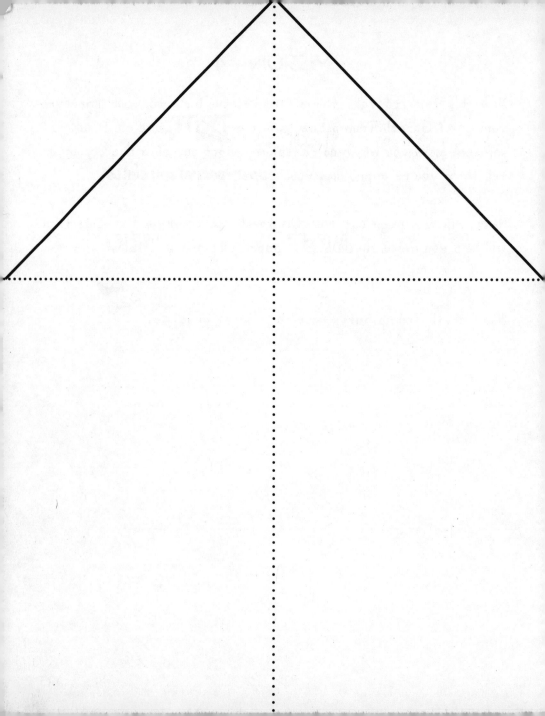